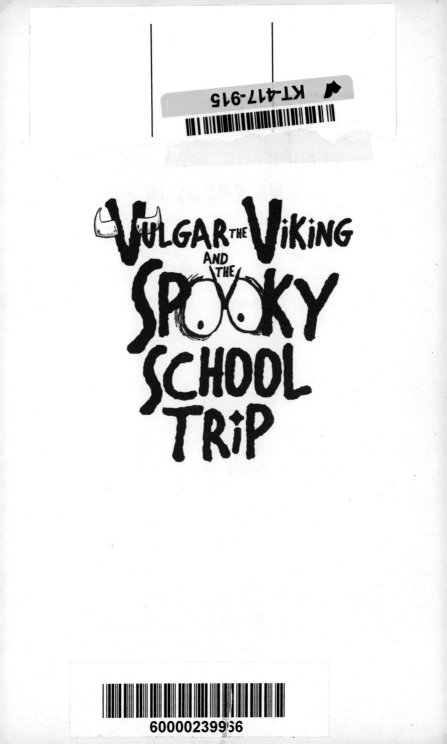

VULGAR THE VIKING
AND THE
SPOOKY
SCHOOL
TRIP

LOOK OUT FOR MORE
STORIES OF MAYHEM
AND CHAOS IN

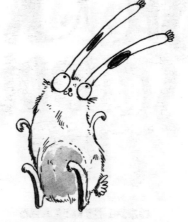

VULGAR THE VIKING
AND THE ROCK CAKE RAIDERS

VULGAR THE VIKING
AND THE GREAT GULP GAMES

VULGAR THE VIKING
AND THE TERRIBLE TALENT SHOW

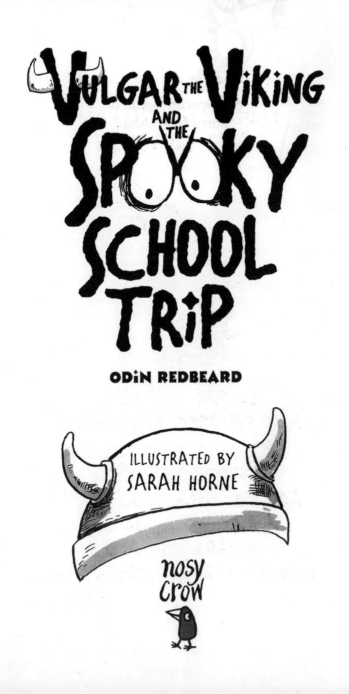

VULGAR THE VIKING AND THE SPOOKY SCHOOL TRIP

ODIN REDBEARD

ILLUSTRATED BY
SARAH HORNE

nosy
crow

First published in the UK in 2012 by Nosy Crow Ltd
The Crow's Nest, 10a Lant St
London, SE1 1QR, UK

Nosy Crow and associated logos are trademarks and/or
registered trademarks of Nosy Crow Ltd

Text copyright © Hothouse Fiction, 2012
Illustrations © Sarah Horne, 2012

The right of Hothouse Fiction and Sarah Horne to be identified as the author
and illustrator respectively of this work has been asserted by them in accordance
with the Copyright, Designs and Patents Act 1988.

A CIP catalogue record for this book will be available from the British Library

Printed and bound in the UK by Clays Ltd, St Ives Plc

Papers used by Nosy Crow are made from wood grown in sustainable forests.

ISBN: 978 0 85763 060 5

www.nosycrow.com

CHAPTER ONE

BACK TO SCHOOL

"Back with you, monster. Back, back!"

Vulgar the Viking swiped with his sword, slashing the air and driving back a slimy sea serpent that had emerged, unexpectedly, from the duck pond in his home village of Blubber.

Around him, the other villagers were running in terror, screaming and wailing as they hurried to safety. Vulgar stood his ground. He tightened his grip on his broadsword and looked the monster in the eye.

"You think you can challenge a *real* Viking?" Vulgar asked. He threw back his head and laughed. "Let me see you try!"

With a *hiss*, the serpent rose up to its full height. It towered above him, blocking out the sun itself. Its terrible jaws opened. The smell of rotten whale meat rolled out, and then the creature spoke in a voice like thunder: "Wakey wakey, sleepyhead."

Vulgar blinked. He lowered his sword.

"Um, what?"

Something shook his shoulders and the sea serpent

vanished in a swirling mist.

Vulgar opened his eyes and saw his mum's face leaning over him. It wasn't as terrifying as the sea monster's face had been, but it was a close run thing.

"Dreaming again?" she asked.

Vulgar nodded sleepily. He should have known it was a dream. Nothing that exciting *ever* happened in Blubber. The scariest thing in Vulgar's village was probably his mum's cooking.

"Which was it this time? The sea serpent or the exploding helmet?"

"The sea serpent," Vulgar said. He tried to hold on to the dream, but it was already fading away. He yawned and pulled the blanket tighter around him. Maybe if he went back to sleep for a while...

"Don't even think about it. You're going to be late as it is," said his mum. Helga was the largest and strongest woman in all of Blubber.

She was stronger than most of the men, too. With one hand she tipped up Vulgar's bed. He screamed with fright as he spilled on to the cold stone floor.

Vulgar looked up in time for a grey tunic to land on his head. "Put that on," Helga told him. "I want you to look smart for your first day back at school."

Five minutes later, Vulgar shuffled into the kitchen and plonked himself down on the bench by the table. His dad, Harald, was there, spreading goat butter on a slice of burnt bread.

Little black crumbs were flying up and getting stuck in his thin, wispy beard.

"Morning, Vulgar," Harald chirped. "Excited about going back to school?"

Vulgar didn't have to think about his answer. "No," he sighed. "Not really."

There was a *clunk* as a piece of blackened toast was put down in front of him. "Eat up," said Helga. "You don't want to be late for class, do you?"

"Well, actually..." said Vulgar.

"Ah, school. The happiest days of your life," said Harald.

Vulgar shuddered. He really hoped that wasn't true.

"You learn so much," Harald continued through a mouthful of burnt bread. "Reading ... er ... other stuff. I wouldn't be where I am today if I hadn't stuck it at school."

"You're a toilet cleaner, dad," Vulgar said.

"Exactly!" cried Harald. "And if you work hard at school, maybe one day you can be a toilet cleaner, too."

"I don't want to be a toilet cleaner, though. I want to be a *real* Viking. I want looting and pillaging, not scrubbing and ... more scrubbing."

Harald looked hurt. "I don't just scrub," he muttered. "I polish, too."

"Viking school should be about proper

Viking stuff," Vulgar sighed. "But try telling that to our teacher."

"Eat," said Helga, snapping off a piece of the bread and shoving it in Vulgar's mouth. "Dagmar the Dull has been Blubber's teacher for as long as I can remember. There's nothing wrong with him."

"Of course there's something wrong with him," said Vulgar, between chews. "He's dull."

"Well, yes," said Helga. "But he's very ... reliable."

Reliably boring, thought Vulgar, but his mouth was too full to say it. A sharp tug at his hair made him yelp and spray crumbs all over Harald. He tried to turn his head, but his mum was holding it steady.

"Don't move or you'll have your eye out," she said, coming at him with

a brush she had made from reindeer antlers. She tugged and pulled at the knots in Vulgar's long, greasy hair but most of them refused to come out, and she was forced to admit defeat.

"That'll have to do," she said, sighing. She handed him his helmet and he pulled it on. Helga had polished the helmet's horns so they gleamed. "Right, off you go to school," she said. "And no getting into trouble!"

"I'll try," said Vulgar. He got up from the table and almost tripped over his flea-bitten dog, Grunt, who was sleeping on the kitchen floor. "Sorry, Grunt," he said, then he carried on out of the house and along the narrow garden path.

His best friend, Knut, was leaning on the gate waiting for him. Vulgar gave his friend a nod of approval. Vulgar was usually scruffy, but Knut always went one better. He slouched as he walked, and his clothes had crumpled to fit his slumped shoulders. His helmet was on the large side, and one of the horns pointed in the wrong direction, because it had snapped off and been stuck back on upside down.

Compared to Knut, Vulgar's half-brushed hair and polished horns made him look like a prince.

"Looking forward to school?" asked Knut.

"No," Vulgar said. "You?"

Knut nodded. "Yeah, I'm really looking forward to it."

Vulgar's jaw dropped open. "What, really?"

"No, not really," said Knut, laughing, and they set off towards the school, walking slowly side by side. They were halfway there when they heard a faint *woof* from behind them.

Vulgar turned to find Grunt following them. The dog wagged his tail happily.

"Go home, Grunt," Vulgar said. "I have to go to school, but you don't. Run. Get away while you still can."

Grunt's tail stopped wagging. He looked from Vulgar to Knut, then back again. Finally, he turned and sloped back off in the direction of the house.

"Wish I could go home," Knut said.

"Yeah," agreed Vulgar. "Me too."

A few minutes later, they arrived inside their classroom. The school was a small stone building with a thatched roof and a strip of mud outside that passed for a playing field. It had just one classroom. A dozen other Viking children were gathered in it. Some of them sat on the benches. Some of them stood leaning against the walls. They all looked just as unhappy as Vulgar felt.

 12

Or *almost* all of them. Princess Freya, daughter of King Olaf, the ruler of Blubber, hopped excitedly from foot to foot. Her long blonde hair was tied in perfect plaits. Her clean white dress spun in frilly circles as she turned on the spot.

Freya was clutching a small wooden longship in her hands and chattering to anyone who would listen.

"I don't know about the rest of you, but I spent most of the holidays on a cruise around the fjords," she said. "It was incredible. Amazing. *Beautiful!*"

"Boring," said Vulgar, with a yawn.

"You're just jealous," Freya sniffed. "Because you've never been on a real longboat before."

She waggled the wooden boat in front of Vulgar's face. "Wow, let's have a look," said Vulgar, grabbing it from her. He held it up and studied it. One day he'd own a boat like that. A real one, too, not just a toy.

"Give it back," Freya demanded. She grabbed for the boat, but Vulgar dodged out of her way.

"I'm just having a look," Vulgar protested, but Freya didn't care. She lunged and snatched the boat back, then stuck her tongue out and flashed Vulgar

a smug smile. Vulgar made to grab
for the boat again, but a familiar voice
stopped him.

"Right, you lot, quit your messin',"
said Harrumf, the crotchety old Viking
who acted as King Olaf's advisor. Vulgar
turned in time to see Harrumf's long
grey beard enter shakily through the

door, followed by the rest of him. "You're expecting to be 'aving Dagmar teaching you, right?" He paused dramatically.

"Wrong!" Harrumf continued. "He won't be 'ere, on account of him havin' been mostly trampled by a moose."

A murmur of excitement went round the group. Dagmar was the only teacher in Blubber. "So does that mean we can go home?" asked Vulgar, hopefully.

"No chance," snapped Harrumf. "We've got a replacement for you."

"It's not you, is it?" said Vulgar.

"You should be so lucky. No, it's someone else. Someone who won't take any of your muckin' about. He's Blubber's most famous son. He's feared in all ten countries in the whole wide world. He's the one, the only..."

Harrumf drummed his fingers against the teacher's desk. "Yes?" mumbled the class.

"...Otto the Bone-Cruncher!"

A wide grin lit up Vulgar's face. Otto the Bone-Cruncher was a *proper* Viking. He was probably the most *proper* Viking who had ever lived.

A hulking shape in an enormous horned helmet ducked in through the door. This was more like it! Maybe school wasn't going to be so bad after all.

CHAPTER TWO

THE FIRST LESSON

"Whoa!" gasped Vulgar, staring up at
the towering Otto. He was the most
impressive-looking Viking Vulgar had
ever seen.

The horns on Otto's helmet were half
a metre long. His beard was so bushy it
looked like it had another beard all of
its own. His eyebrows were like angry
caterpillars having a fight, and his arms

were like tree trunks with
fists attached to the end.
He didn't just look big,
he made the rest of the
room look small.

"This is going to be *amazing*," Vulgar blurted out, grinning. Otto's glare moved down and stopped on him. The big Viking's nostrils flared.

"You bet your scrawny wee boots it will!" he bellowed in a voice like an avalanche. "Now sit down. All of you. Quickly, so you don't miss any of the amazing things I've got to say."

It took less than a second for every single pupil to sit down on one of the classroom benches. Otto's voice was still ringing in their ears, and none of them wanted to get on the big man's bad side.

"Call that quick?" Otto scoffed. "My grandmother could move quicker than that. And she's got no legs."

The class looked up at him in silence. Somewhere near the back of the room, the sheer volume of Otto's voice made one of the younger boys cry. Otto raced

20

over to him, hoisted him up by the back of his tunic, then tossed him out through the window.

"There'll be no blubberers in *my* class," he told the rest of them, as he stomped back to the front of the room.

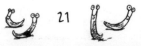

"But we're all Blubberers," Vulgar pointed out. "We're from Blubber."

Otto glared down at Vulgar, his eyes bulging, his face going an angry shade of purple. Before he could start shouting, though, Harrumf interrupted.

"Right. I'll leave you in Otto's capable hands," the old man said. He turned and hobbled out of the room. Otto watched him leave, shot Vulgar another angry look, then turned to the rest of the pupils.

"This school thing," he said. "Waste of time. Reading runes. *Counting?* That's not what real Vikings do. I've never counted higher than three in my entire life. You don't need to when you're fighting dragons. If you haven't killed it after three sword slices, you're dead. One, two, three. That's all you need to know."

Vulgar leaned closer. He was liking the sound of this.

"So from now on forget all that stuff," Otto continued. "I'm going to teach you babies how to be *real* Vikings. I'm going to toughen you up and teach you how to survive. None of this reading rubbish."

Freya raised a hand. "Can we talk about what we did during the summer holidays?" she asked, hopefully.

"No!" thundered Otto.

"But I went on a cruise and—"

"I don't care! Do you know what I did

in the holidays?"

"What?" asked Vulgar, breathlessly.

"I tamed a polar bear, headbutted a giant and conquered Norway."

"You headbutted a giant?" Vulgar gasped. He was impressed. The most exciting thing he'd done in the holidays was sleep.

Otto puffed out his chest. "I headbutt a giant at least once a day," he announced. "And twice on Sundays."

"Can you teach us how to headbutt a giant?" Vulgar asked.

"No!" boomed Otto. "You're all too titchy. You wouldn't reach."

"Can you teach us swordfighting, then?"

Otto's eyes narrowed. "Swordfighting?" he said, standing over Vulgar's desk and glaring down. "You want me to teach you *swordfighting*?"

Vulgar gulped. "Um ... yes."

The big Viking gave a nod. "An excellent idea."

A little while later, the whole class stood in the small courtyard outside the school. They had each been given a short wooden sword, and then ordered to copy what Otto did.

The teacher drew his own sword – a heavy steel blade that was easily as long as Vulgar's whole body – and began frantically chopping and stabbing at the air with it.

"You do this, and then you do this, and then you give it some of *that*," Otto said, hacking and slashing at an invisible opponent. "And then, when they least expect it, you let them have a taste of *this* and one of *these*, and then a couple of *those* for luck."

He slid his sword back into its scabbard. "Everyone got that?"

The pupils all blinked and mumbled uncertainly.

"Good. You'll work in pairs," Otto told them.

Vulgar grinned and went to team up with Knut, but a big hand caught him by the tunic and hoisted him off the ground. "You can fight her," Otto said, dropping

Vulgar beside Freya.

"What?" Vulgar spluttered. "But why?"

Otto stroked his wild beard. "Let me think. Oh, yes. *Because I said so!* Everyone else, pair up and show me what you're made of."

As the teacher strode off to shout some more at other people, Vulgar turned to Freya. "Get ready to see what a real Viking is made of," he warned her.

THONK!

"Ouch!" he yelped, covering his head with his arms.

PRONK!

"Oof!" he cried, bringing his hands down to protect his ribs.

DONK!

Vulgar leapt backwards. "Cut it out," he said. "I wasn't ready."

Freya lowered her wooden weapon. "Fine," she sighed. "Are you ready now?"

Vulgar gripped the handle of his own sword. He nodded. "Ready."

THONK!

"Ow!"

Freya laughed. "Some real Viking you are. You can't even beat a girl."

That did it. With a roar of anger, Vulgar ran at the princess, his sword swinging. She sidestepped at the very last moment, and Vulgar crashed face first into the teacher's bum.

Otto turned to see Vulgar stumbling backwards then falling to the ground. The teacher stepped over Vulgar and glared down at him.

Vulgar gave a groan. "Is it playtime yet?"

"*Playtime?*" Otto laughed. He slapped his thigh with one plate-sized hand. "Real Vikings don't play. There will be no *play*time from now on."

An unhappy murmur went through the class. Knut raised a hand. "What about lunch?" he asked. "We still get lunch, right?"

Vulgar's stomach gave a worried grumble.

"No playtime," Otto said. "And no lunch, either."

Vulgar's face went pale. "But we'll starve!"

"Nonsense," Otto said. "I once went for six years eating only tree bark and dust. Lunch is cancelled. Lunch is for wimps!"

Down on the ground, Vulgar gave another groan. No playtime, and now no lunch? He suddenly wished he'd eaten more of the burnt toast at breakfast. If only someone had told him that being a proper Viking was going to be such hungry work.

CHAPTER THREE

SOMETHING'S BURNING

The next day, Vulgar and Knut made their way to school. Vulgar was limping. Freya had turned out to be a lot better with a sword than she looked. Still, Vulgar's bruises didn't make him any less excited about the day ahead.

"I wonder what we'll learn today?" he said.

Knut shrugged. "Dunno."

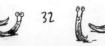

32

"Looting, probably," Vulgar said. "Or plundering. Maybe a bit of pillaging, if we're lucky."

The day's lesson was on none of these things, however. The boys arrived at school to find a fire burning in the courtyard. Otto explained – with lots of shouting – that he was going to teach them how to light fires using just a sword and a stone.

"All *right!*" cheered Vulgar, punching the air with delight. His mum would never let him light a fire in a million years, not since he'd accidentally set her hair alight with that candle on his last birthday.

Starting the fire wasn't as easy as it looked. It took Vulgar almost an hour of hitting the stone with the sword to produce even one small spark. The others weren't having much luck, either, except

 33

Freya who had managed to get a roaring fire going after just a few minutes.

Otto paced around the class, snapping and roaring at every pupil in turn. Say what you liked about the big Viking, he was fair. He shouted at everyone equally.

"Get a move on!" he said, as Vulgar tried for the three hundredth time to get his fire lit. There was barely anything left of his stone now, and the blade of the sword was bent and blunt. He wiped the sweat from his forehead, and had another go.

The blade hit the side of the stone and a flash of orange filled Vulgar's vision. He blinked, then looked down at the bundle of straw beside the stone, hoping to see it smouldering.

Nothing.

He sniffed. There *was* a burning smell, though. It was coming from somewhere close by. Somewhere *very* close by.

"Hey, Vulgar," Knut called. "I think your hair is on fire."

"What?" said Vulgar.

"Yep, definitely on fire."

Vulgar looked up and saw smoke curling from his tufts of hair. A moment later, he felt his forehead begin to burn.

Vulgar dropped his sword and began slapping himself hard on the head. "Put it out! Put it out!" he yelped, then gasped as a bucket of freezing cold water was thrown into his face.

He turned, shivering, his teeth chattering together, and found Freya smiling at him. She had an empty bucket in her hand. "Wow," she said. "Who knew being the school fire marshall could be so much fun?"

"T-t-towel," Vulgar stammered. "G-give me a t-towel."

"A towel?" boomed Otto. He shook his head. "You'll dry in the air, boy. Towels are for wimps!"

By Wednesday, Vulgar wasn't quite as excited about school. He still had the bruises from Monday and had only just warmed up from his soaking.

He was even less excited when he and Knut turned up to find the teacher's table groaning under the weight of ... well, he wasn't really sure what the things on the table were. Some of them were lumpy. Some of them were squidgy. Almost all of them were brown.

"Poo," announced Otto. "When you're in the wilderness, you can identify an animal by looking at its poo."

"Looking at its *poo*?" Freya groaned.

"And smelling it," Otto added.

"I think I'm going to be sick," Knut said, clamping a hand over his mouth.

"Nonsense," Otto roared. He clicked his fingers and pointed to Vulgar. "You," he said. "Come up here and pick a poo."

Vulgar stood up and slowly approached the table. His eyes went from brown lump to brown lump, trying to decide if any looked less disgusting than the rest. But they were all just as disgusting as each other. Juggling dried elk poo was one of Vulgar's favourite pastimes, but this poo was soft and wet and *fresh*. Yuck.

"That one," he said, picking a large smelly splodge at random.

"Right. And what animal do you think

left that little present behind?" Otto asked.

Vulgar shrugged. He wrinkled his nose and peered down at the mound. It was easily the size of the loaf his mum had baked at breakfast, and smelled almost as bad. "Hedgehog?"

"*Hedgehog?*" Otto snorted. "Look at the size of it! It's twice the size of a hedgehog, boy. Get your hand in and have a squidge around. See if you can find any clues."

Vulgar hesitated. Then he heard the rest of the class gasp as he slid his hand into the sticky brown sludge.

It felt unpleasantly warm. The smell that came from within it made his head spin.

There was a sound like someone choking, and Freya gave a sudden scream. All eyes looked to the princess. She was sitting at her desk looking horrified. Sick dribbled down her plaits and on to her dress.

Knut stood behind her, wiping his mouth on his sleeve. "Sorry," he said, quietly. "I couldn't hold that in any longer."

Even though he was up to his wrist in poo, Vulgar giggled.

Otto shook his head. "All right," he muttered. "Let's leave the poo lesson for another day."

Vulgar breathed a sigh of relief and pulled his hand free with a *schlop*. He held the hand out to Otto. "Now can I get a towel or something?"

"Didn't you listen yesterday?" cried Otto. "Towels are for *wimps!*"

When Thursday came around, Vulgar was pretty fed up. He'd been excited about learning to be a real Viking, but none of it had quite worked out the way he'd hoped.

The smell of animal poo wouldn't come off his hand. He'd even tried washing it – in actual water! No matter how hard he scrubbed, the smell hadn't disappeared.

He was beginning to worry it would *never* come off and he'd smell like his dad for ever.

Still, today was going to be better. Otto had said something about them building their own armour. That was more like it. Vulgar had a spring in his step that lasted all the way to school.

The excitement didn't last once he'd arrived.

"Sewing?" he gasped. "*Thor's nostrils*, you want us to sew stuff? Since when did Vikings sew stuff?"

Otto drew himself up to his full impressive height. "A true Viking always sews his own armour," the teacher said. "How can you trust armour you haven't made yourself?"

"But ... but ... *sewing*?"

"Freya has already put together a most impressive outfit," Otto said.

Vulgar turned to find the princess
modelling a suit of leather armour,
complete with gloves, boots and
even a little
mask that
attached to a
horned helmet.

"Well, of course she has," Vulgar muttered. "She's a girl. Girls sew. Vikings don't."

"Oh, really?" growled Otto, bringing his huge bearded face down to Vulgar's level. "For that you can stay behind after school and darn the holes in all my old socks."

"What?" coughed Vulgar.

"And then after that," said Otto, scowling, "you can start on my pants."

Vulgar didn't want to go to school on Friday. Between the bruises, the freezing water, the stinky poo and the stinkier pants, he'd had enough. He  tried pretending to be sick, but then his mum brought out the big bottle of thick brown medicine she'd made from boiled tree roots. He'd take school over that medicine any day, and quickly made a full recovery.

In the end, he was glad he went. Otto said he was tired of seeing them all mess up the Viking lessons, and that they were going to do something easier. A true Viking, he explained, should always be able to tell stories around the campfire.

To demonstrate, he told them about the time he'd fended off an invading army using just his elbows and one foot.

Then he told them to write their own stories, which they would get a chance to share with the rest of the class at the end of the day.

Otto sat at his desk and sharpened his broadsword while the pupils started writing. Vulgar usually hated writing stories, but compared to the rest of the week, he found himself really enjoying it.

He wrote a story about a killer troll eating a teacher. It was very detailed, from the first hungry growls of the monster to the big happy *burp* it made at the end of the meal.

"Right, who wants to read their story out?" asked Otto when the end of the day arrived.

Vulgar stood up before anyone else had the chance. "Mine's called *The Flesh-Eating Troll*," he announced.

Otto cleared his throat. "Maybe

someone else should go first."

Vulgar ignored the suggestion, and launched into the story. "Once upon a time, there was a flesh-eating troll."

"A troll?" said Otto. He swallowed.

"Yes, a big flesh-eating beast of a troll."

"Flesh-eating...?" Otto said. He was looking a bit pale.

"Yes, a real monster," Vulgar continued. "With huge arms, and pointy teeth and—"

Otto swung with his sword and it *clanged* against a bell that was fixed to the wall. "School's over," he said quickly.

A cheer went up from the other pupils and they all jumped to their feet. Vulgar looked down at his story. "But I'd just started."

Otto shrugged. "And now you're finished."

Vulgar frowned. He'd been looking forward to telling the story. "He's in a big rush to get out of here," Vulgar grumbled to Knut.

"Hey, cheer up," said Knut. "It's the weekend. Two whole days of no school."

Vulgar smiled. That *had* cheered him up. He joined the rest of the class in rushing towards the door, but Otto stepped into their path.

"Before you go, I've got a treat for you," he said. "Tomorrow we're going to put everything we've learned this week into practice."

Knut scratched his head. "What do you mean?"

A broad smile spread behind Otto's wild beard. "We're going on a school camping trip. Then we'll see if any of you has what it takes to be a *real* Viking!"

"But tomorrow's the weekend," Vulgar objected.

"The weekend?" Otto snorted. He shook his head. "Weekends are for wimps!"

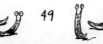

CHAPTER FOUR

SLUG SURPRISE

The next morning Vulgar bounded
out of bed, looking forward to his usual
Saturday routine of playing and relaxing.
But then he remembered: the camping
trip! Before Vulgar knew it he was saying
goodbye to his mum and dad, and giving
Grunt a farewell pat on the head.

"See you tomorrow, boy," he said.

Grunt gave a sad *woof* in reply.

50

"Don't worry, I'll be back before you know it." Vulgar pointed to a hill a few miles from the village. "See that mountain? That's where we're going," he said. "Knut says there are trolls up there, like the one from my story. Maybe we'll get lucky and they'll eat Otto."

With a final pat for Grunt, Vulgar set off. Even though he'd had to give up the weekend, he was actually pretty excited about the trip. He was setting off into the wilderness like a proper Viking would. It was just what he'd always wanted.

The only problem was Otto. The thought of spending a whole two days in the company of Otto the Bone-Cruncher worried him. Proper Viking or not, the man was clearly a loony.

"Get a move on," Otto roared, when all the children had arrived at school. Vulgar fell into step next to Knut.

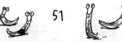

They took up position at the back of the line, as Otto led the class towards the foot of the hill.

Vulgar's knapsack was bulging with stuff his mum had made him take. He had three changes of underwear, six pairs of socks and a toothbrush made from a whalebone.

Knut, on the other hand, was carrying nothing. Despite this, he still walked slower than Vulgar. Otto had not failed to notice this.

"Hurry up at the back," shouted the teacher, and the boys reluctantly sped up.

The climb was hard work. By the end of the first hour, everyone's legs were aching. No one dared complain, though, in case they brought the full wrath of Otto down upon themselves.

Otto himself seemed to be having the time of his life. He marched on ahead, pumping his arms, breathing in deeply through his nose.

"Look," he said, pointing to the ground. "Animal tracks. Can anyone tell me what animal made those?"

"Fox?" suggested one of the pupils.

"Bear?" guessed another.

Otto shook his head. "Elephant," he said.

Most of the pupils stared at him blankly. Some of them nodded, as if they'd known this all along.

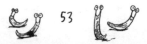

"What's an elephant?" asked
Vulgar.

"You don't
know what an
elephant is?"
chuckled
Otto. "An
elephant,
as everyone
knows, is a

ferocious creature with six legs, big claws
and ... two mouths."

Vulgar frowned. "Two mouths?"

"Yes," said Otto firmly. "Eight legs,
sharp claws, and two mouths."

"You said they had six legs," Vulgar
said.

Otto narrowed his eyes. "They ... grow
more," he said. "When they get older.
Now, let's press on."

He about-turned before Vulgar could

ask any more questions and the group carried on up the hill. Vulgar looked down at the footprints in the mud as they passed. So those were elephant footprints, were they? Funny, he would've sworn they belonged to a dog.

They climbed on for another four hours, winding their way around the hill as they made for the summit.

"This is *not* fun," wheezed Knut. "I'd rather be in class studying runes."

Vulgar nodded. "I'd rather be *anywhere*."

"How much further?" shouted Freya, who was somewhere near the middle of the group.

"Not far now," bellowed Otto. A sigh of relief went around the pupils. "Another hour or so and we'll be almost halfway."

"*Halfway!*" gasped Vulgar. "We've been walking for ever!"

Otto must have heard him, because the

teacher stopped suddenly, making the pupils directly behind him crash into his back. "Right," he said, "let's stop for a drink."

Vulgar let out a happy yelp. There was a little stream near where they were walking. The water was crystal clear. Vulgar licked his dry lips. "A drink?" he said. "We can really stop for a drink?"

"Of course you can," Otto nodded. "It's important to stay hydrated."

"Whoo-hoo!" cried Vulgar. He and Knut began racing towards the stream, but a sudden shout from Otto stopped them.

"Where do you think you're going?"

"The stream," said Vulgar. "To get a drink."

Otto's eyebrows raised. "Who said anything about the stream? There's dew on the grass. You can lick that off."

Vulgar looked down at the grass. "You *can't* be serious."

"I'm always serious," Otto told him. "If you're thirsty, you can lick the wet grass."

"But ... there's a stream."

"Ha!" laughed Otto, and the sound rolled down the hill. "That's the easy way. Real Vikings *never* take the easy way. Real Vikings do things the hard way, and if there is no hard way they don't do it at all. Streams are for—"

"Wimps," Vulgar finished. "We get it."

Knut and Vulgar exchanged a glance. Then, without another word, they both got down on their knees and began to lick the water off the grass.

"So," said Knut between licks, "do you think Otto's mad or what?"

"I hope so," said Vulgar, scraping a bug off his tongue. "Because if this is what being a real Viking is all about, I don't think I'll bother!"

Once they'd all had a drink, Otto led them the rest of the way up the hill. They finally reached the top just as the sky was going dark, and set about building a shelter.

The whole class worked on the shelter, fetching sticks, binding them together and covering them with branches and bracken.

"Ta-daa!" said Vulgar, putting the

last stick in place and stepping back to admire their handiwork. "I think that looks—"

There was a *creaking* of wood, and the entire shelter collapsed in on itself like a house of cards.

"—rubbish," Vulgar sighed.

Freya took control of the second attempt. She stood at the side, bossing everyone around and prodding them with a stick if they moved too slowly. In no time the shelter had been rebuilt, and this time it stayed built.

"Dinner time," Otto announced. He held up something small, dark and squidgy. "Slug surprise. We'll cook them over the campfire."

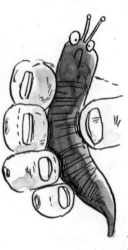

"We haven't got a campfire," Freya pointed out.

Otto stared at her. "Well, you'd better light one."

Grumbling, Freya set about lighting a fire. The rest of the class lined up in front of Otto. He grinned as he handed each of them one fat slug.

"What's the surprise part?" asked Freya.

"The surprise is they taste even worse than you expect," Otto told her.

"Suppose we'd better go and get ours," Knut said. Knut would eat pretty much anything, but even he didn't look happy about the slug surprise.

"Don't worry," said Vulgar. He rummaged in his knapsack and pulled out some strips of dried reindeer meat. "I brought these. No slugs for us!"

Knut almost cheered, but Vulgar put a hand over his mouth. "Keep it down," Vulgar warned. "We don't want old Bone-Cruncher finding out."

"Finding out what?" asked Freya, bobbing up beside them.

"Nothing," said Vulgar, hiding the dried meat behind his back. "I thought you were lighting the fire?"

"I already have," Freya said. "Is that food? Give me some."

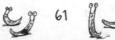

"No!" Vulgar hissed.

Freya raised a hand. "Sir," she began, "Vulgar's got—"

"Ssh! OK, fine. You can have some." Vulgar thrust a strip of meat into Freya's hands. "But don't tell anyone else."

A little while later, full of reindeer meat, Vulgar, Knut and Freya joined the others around the campfire.

Otto held out a bowl of squidgy grey goop. "Slug surprise?"

"No thanks," said Vulgar. "We're not going to eat anything."

"Food's for wimps," said Knut, then he burped quietly.

Otto nodded approvingly. "Good boys. Now, who wants to tell us a campfire tale?"

"Me!" said Vulgar, jumping up. This was his chance to tell his troll story.

"Once upon a time, there was a flesh-eating troll. It lived high on a hillside, much like this one."

The flames crackled higher and silence fell over the camp as everyone listened to Vulgar's tale.

"Most of the time, the troll left people alone. If people didn't bother him, then he didn't bother them. But sometimes, on nights just like this, the townsfolk

would head off into the hills. Camping."

"Camping?" whispered Otto.

"Camping," said Vulgar.

Otto's eyes darted left and right into the gloom. "On ... on nights like this?"

"Exactly like this," said Vulgar. "The campers would accidentally wander too close to his house and hunger would take control of him."

"Hunger?" said Otto. His voice came out as a high-pitched squeak.

"Yes, hunger," continued Vulgar. "He'd leap out, his huge teeth snapping at—"

"Right, dinner's over," said Otto. "Time for bed."

"What? But I haven't finished."

Otto ignored him. The teacher stood up and kicked dirt into the fire, putting it out. Darkness fell on the hillside. "Everyone into the shelter," he said. "Anyone who isn't asleep in five minutes will be in big trouble. Hurry, hurry!"

Muttering, Vulgar joined the others as they filed into the shelter. The ground was uncomfortable as he lay down on it, and the rock he was using for a pillow wasn't doing his head any favours at all.

From somewhere in the darkness, he heard a whimpering. *Freya*, he guessed. She lived in the castle and wasn't used to roughing it like this. She'd *never* make a proper Viking.

Gradually, Vulgar's eyes began to close. Some of the other children were already sleeping. At last, with the sound of Knut's snoring rattling in his ears, Vulgar managed to fall asleep.

"AAAAAAAARGH!"

Vulgar opened his eyes and sat up. "Wha—?"

The scream had come from somewhere in the corner of the shelter. Vulgar sat up as whoever was over there shouted again.

"Troll! Help, help, there's a troll out there!" wailed the voice. "And it's going to eat us all up!"

CHAPTER FIVE

THE TROLL REVEALED

There was the sound of metal hitting stone, and Freya sparked up a flaming torch. The light of the fire revealed Otto cowering in the corner of the shelter. The teacher was wearing yellow woolly pyjamas. His big hands were holding something tightly to his chest.

"Is that ... is that a teddy bear?" Vulgar asked.

"Troll!"
Otto
whimpered.
Freya frowned.
"It doesn't look like
a troll."
"I'm pretty sure it's a teddy
bear," Vulgar said.

"Not Mr Cuddles, out there," Otto sobbed. "Listen. Can't you hear it?"

The whole class was awake now. They all held their breath and listened. For a long time they heard nothing, but then came a rustling and a cracking of twigs from right outside the shelter.

"See," said Otto in a soft whisper. A tear ran down his cheek and he hugged Mr Cuddles tighter. "It's a flesh-eating troll, like the one in that horrible story of yours!"

"Really? Brilliant!" Vulgar cheered.

"Are you going to battle it?"

"Don't be silly, I made that up!" Otto sobbed. "Someone get it away. We're all going to be eaten!"

Freya shook her head. "Some Viking he turned out to be."

The sound outside the shelter came again. It sounded louder this time. Whatever was out there was trying to get inside.

"He's right, it's going to eat us," whispered one of Vulgar's classmates.

"What do we do?" mumbled another.

Otto got to his feet. "I know what I'm going to do," he said. "Run awaaaaay!"

With a *crash*, the big teacher charged straight through the wall. The shelter was filled with screaming as the rest of the pupils raced out after him, trying to escape whatever was trying to force its way inside.

Vulgar and Freya listened to the wailing of the children, and the even louder wailing of Otto. Down on the floor, Knut snored loudly.

"Can he sleep through *anything*?" Freya asked.

Vulgar nodded and gave his friend a nudge. "Pretty much."

Knut rubbed his eyes. "What's happening? Where is everyone?"

"They think there's a troll outside," Vulgar explained. "They all ran away."

Knut nodded. "Oh. Right," he said, then he turned over and tried to go back to sleep.

"Get up," Freya barked. "What if a troll really *is* trying to eat us?"

"Then I'd rather sleep through it," Knut grumbled, but he stood up anyway.

The rustling was right outside the hole in the wall now. Vulgar, Knut and Freya drew closer together, their eyes trained on the gap.

"It's coming," Freya whispered.

"It might not be too bad," Vulgar said. "It might eat you first."

Freya punched him on the arm, but kept her gaze fixed on the hole.

Something was moving there, just outside

the shelter. Something that definitely wasn't human.

With a jolly hop, a rabbit appeared in the gap. Its little nose twitched as it sniffed the air.

The children stared down at the bunny, with its long ears and fluffy white tail. Then they burst out laughing.

"That's the cutest troll I've ever seen," said Freya. She gave the rabbit a pat on the head. It twitched its nose again, flicked its ears, then hopped back out into the darkness.

"Can I go back to sleep now?" yawned Knut.

Vulgar shook his head. "No. I think we should go home. I've had enough of camping."

73

"Me too," agreed Freya.

Knut shrugged. "OK. Lead the way."

A full moon hung over the hill when they stepped outside. It cast a spooky white glow across the grass, giving them just enough light to see by. Vulgar peered into the gloom, deep in thought.

"What's the problem?" asked Freya.

"I'm trying to decide which way we should go."

"Well, *down* might be a good place to start," said the princess. She pushed past

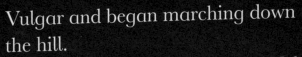

Vulgar and began marching down
the hill.

"I know we need to go *down*," Vulgar
said, as he and Knut trudged after her,
"but we might be going down the wrong
side."

Freya shook her head. "We aren't."

"How do you know?"

The princess stopped suddenly and
pointed up at the sky. "Look at the
stars," she said. Knut and Vulgar
looked up. A thousand white
dots filled the night above
them.

"Yeah, nice," said
Vulgar. "So?"

"So the stars
can help us
get home.

The village is to the north, so we follow the North Star. I thought a *real* Viking would know that?"

"Of course I did," Vulgar replied. He looked up. "Which one's the North Star again?"

Freya hesitated.

"You don't know, do you?" Vulgar said with a smirk.

"I do so!" Freya replied. "It's that one."

"Well, I think it's *that* one," Vulgar argued. "What do you think, Knut?"

Knut gave a snore.

"He's standing up," Freya said. "How can he be sleeping standing up?"

With a splutter, Knut woke up again. "Five more minutes, Mum," he said, loudly, then he realised where he was and gave an embarassed cough. "Sorry about that," he said. "Carry on."

"You two are hopeless," Freya said. "I'll

find my way home myself." She began marching down the hill to the left. Vulgar and Knut watched her go.

"Should we follow her?" Knut asked, eventually.

"No way," said Vulgar. "She'll never find her way home. It's this way." He began walking down the hill to the right. "Stick with me, Knut, and we'll be home in no time."

They walked for an hour or more, stumbling and sliding through the damp grass as they made their way down the hill. To pass the time, Vulgar told Knut the ending of his troll story.

"The children screamed and ran through the darkness, the troll's big feet shaking the hillside – *boom, boom, boom* – as it gave chase."

Vulgar stopped walking and Knut

bumped into his back. "Then the footsteps stopped." Vulgar's voice lowered to a whisper. "And the campers realised that the troll wasn't behind them any longer. It was in front of them…"

"In front?" Knut gulped.

"*Right* in front."

Both boys held their breath. Vulgar's belly filled with butterflies. His story was so scary he'd frightened himself.

"This is just a story, right?" Knut whimpered.

"Yeah," said Vulgar, although suddenly he didn't feel so sure. "It's just a story."

The boys exchanged a glance. "You think we should run?" whispered Knut. "Just in case?"

Vulgar nodded. "I think we should run."

And with that, both boys ran. They raced down the hillside, their feet tangling in the damp grass. Vulgar heard a *boom, boom, boom* from somewhere close by. For a moment he thought it was a giant's footsteps, then he realised it was the sound of his heart pounding in his chest.

Suddenly, something moved in the gloom right in front of them. Vulgar just had time to scream, "TROLL!", before his head smacked against it. Stars twinkled behind his eyes as he fell over.

"Ow!" said a voice that was very un-troll-like. The last thing Vulgar saw before he fell unconscious was Freya's angry face looming down at him from above.

CHAPTER SIX

CHASED THROUGH THE DARKNESS

Vulgar was woken up by a slap across the face. He blinked open his eyes in time to see Freya's hand come swishing towards him again.

"Cut it out!" he cried, rolling to safety. "I'm awake! Stop hitting me. Haven't you done enough damage?"

"What are you doing here?" Freya demanded. "Were you following me?"

"No way," said Vulgar, standing up. "You were following us."

"Ha, in your dreams," Freya said. "I was following *that* star."

"Well, we were following *that* one," Vulgar told her.

Freya sighed. "It's the same star, Vulgar."

"No it isn't," Vulgar argued. He looked more closely. "Oh, wait, so it is. Well, we were following it first."

"Uh, guys," said Knut.

"You were not! I said that's the one *I* was following."

Vulgar scowled. "No you didn't, you were following *that* one."

Freya's voice raised. "That's still the same star!"

"Guys..."

"I wasn't pointing at that one," Vulgar said.

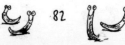

Freya clenched her fists. "Yes you were!"

"GUYS!"

Vulgar and Freya turned to Knut. "*What?*"

Knut put his finger to his lips. "Listen."

A twig snapped somewhere nearby. Something swished through the grass.

"What was that?" Vulgar whispered.

Freya shook her head. "Oh, stop being such a baby. It's probably another bunny."

A series of loud snuffling and snorting sounds came from a little further up the hill. Even in the moonlight, Vulgar saw Freya's face go white.

"Or maybe not," she squeaked.

A low, rumbling growl
filled the gloom behind them.
All three children began to run at
exactly the same time. They raced down
the hill as fast as they could. They didn't
care any longer which direction they
were going, as long as it was away from
the snuffling thing in the darkness.

"We're going to get eaten by a troll,"
Freya yelped. "This is officially the worst
school trip ever."

"Don't talk. Just run!" Vulgar told her.
He pointed towards a clump of trees.

"There. That way. We can climb up."

"Can't trolls climb?" Knut asked.

Vulgar had no idea. He hoped not. "We'll soon find out," he said.

They sprinted for the woods, tripping and stumbling through the long grass. The thing in the darkness came running after them, snuffling and growling with every step it took.

It took them less than a minute to reach the trees, but their hopes were dashed when they got there.

"The branches are too high," Freya sobbed. "We can't reach them!"

Vulgar stood at the base of one of the larger trees. "Here, I'll give you a boost, then you can pull me up."

Freya didn't wait to be asked again. She clambered up Vulgar, caught hold of the lowest branch and pulled herself up.

"Now you, Knut," said Vulgar. Knut put his foot in Vulgar's hands. Straining, Vulgar helped lift his friend until he was high enough to reach the branch.

"Now you," Knut said, as he and Freya both reached down. Vulgar stretched up. His fingers brushed against Freya's, but then something large and heavy slammed into him from the side, sending him crashing down on to the forest floor.

Vulgar heard Knut cry out. He heard Freya scream with shock. Then he heard the troll give a happy bark, before it licked him right on the lips.

"Grunt?" Vulgar spluttered. "Is that you?"

The shaggy dog barked again. There was a rustling sound from above them as Knut fell out of the tree.

"Whoa," he muttered, sitting up and

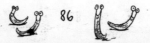

rubbing his head. "I fell asleep again."

Grunt gave Knut a slobbery lick.

"If we're not about to be eaten alive, someone get me down," demanded Freya from up in the branches. Knut and Vulgar looked at each other.

"Should we leave her?" Knut asked.

Vulgar grinned. "Tempting."

"Don't you dare!" Freya warned them.

"All right, all right," grumbled Vulgar. He gave Grunt a final pat and got to his feet. He held out his arms and peered up into the tree. "Jump. I'll catch you."

Freya hesitated, but then Vulgar heard the branches above him creak. "OK. Are you beneath me? I can't see you in the dark."

"I'm right beneath you," said Vulgar. "Hurry up!"

There was a short scream and Freya crashed to the ground on the other side of the tree. Vulgar looked over at her, then he pointed up into the dark foliage.

"Sorry," he said. "Accident. I thought that was you there."

Freya jumped up. Her face was splattered with mud and she had strands of grass and several twigs in her long blonde hair.

"You did that on purpose!" she snapped.

"Me?" said Vulgar,

innocently. "I'd never do a thing like that."

"Hey, look," said Knut, interrupting them before they could start fighting. "I think Grunt's trying to tell us something."

All eyes turned to the dog. He was backing away from the group, wagging his tail excitedly.

"What is it, boy?" asked Vulgar. Grunt ran in a circle, darted a few steps down the hill, then turned and ran back. "Do you want us to follow you?"

Grunt barked loudly.

"Does that mean 'yes'?" asked Freya.

Vulgar shrugged. "I have no idea. But I *think* he's going to lead us home."

And he did. The three children fell in line behind the shaggy dog as he made his way down the hill. It was still dark, but Grunt's sense of smell made sure they were walking in the right direction.

After fifteen minutes or so, they came across the rest of their class. The children were all huddled together, crying and complaining about being lost.

"Where's Otto?" asked Vulgar, as Freya set about organising the pupils into pairs, making them line up behind Grunt.

"He ran off," said a small girl near the front. "Crying for his mummy."

Vulgar and Knut laughed. So much for the big tough *proper* Viking.

They set off again all together, with Grunt at the front and a long line of children following close behind. The sun was starting to come up as they finally made it back to Blubber.

When they drew close to the village they saw a large group of worried parents standing around outside the Great Hall. As soon as the parents saw the children they ran to meet them, whooping and

 90

cheering with relief.

Firm hands caught hold of Vulgar and his mum pulled him into a great big bearhug. "You're OK," she said. "We were so worried."

"Why?" wheezed Vulgar, because his mum's bearhugs always took his breath away. "We weren't due back until later."

"I spotted that Otto running through town when I was on my way to work," said Vulgar's dad. "Screaming something about a troll, he was."

Vulgar looked down at Grunt. "Oh yeah, the troll. It turned out to be quite friendly in the end."

King Olaf strode over to join them, leading a very messy Freya by the hand. "I'm afraid Otto will no longer be your teacher," he said. "He told me he had to go and conquer Denmark at once. In his pyjamas, apparently."

Every one of the children cheered at that, but Vulgar cheered loudest of all. No teacher meant no school. From here on, life would just be one long holiday.

"But don't worry," said King Olaf. "You'll be pleased to hear that Dagmar the Dull is back on his feet, and he'll be back teaching you as of Monday."

Vulgar groaned. Not Dagmar the Dull.

Still, after the week they'd had with Otto, maybe there was something to be said for boring old school work, after all.